SEALED WITH A KISS

MIDNIGHT DELTA SERIES
A NOVELLA

BY CAITLYN O'LEARY

Keep up with Caitlyn and sign up for her newsletter:
http://bit.ly/1WIhRup

DEDICATION

To all of us who are nervous and need reassurance.
Remember people you love will always have your back.

SYNOPSIS

When Billy Anderson decided to ask Rebecca Barnes to the Valentine's Day Dance, he had no idea he would be getting advice from six Navy SEALs. All of the men mean well, and some of them really do help, but his real issue is Rebecca.

There is more going on with Rebecca than she is willing to share. She needs help. The men of Midnight Delta will go above and beyond the call of duty to help the young woman Billy cares for. Will they be able to make sure that Rebecca is safe and happy?

Can the advice of Drake, Mason, Darius, Finn, Clint, and Jack help Billy and Rebecca have the Valentine's Day of their dreams?

This book contains adult content and is meant for ages eighteen and older.

CHAPTER ONE

Billy Anderson

He watched his sister rushing to the back of the diner as she took another order. She was in her element. It used to bother him, seeing her working so hard, but Mason, her fiancé, had made him realize this was part of what made her happy. She came back out holding a pot of coffee.

She had a bright smile for him as she breezed by the table where he was doing his homework.

"Hi Billy, how's it going? Do you have any questions? Darius is going to be here soon. He should be able to help."

"Nope, I'm covered." She made as if to fluff his hair, and then stopped herself. *Thank God.* He was going to be fourteen next month.

She went to top off the coffee for some of the regular customers, and take the orders of people he hadn't seen before. He went back to his social studies homework. He loved social studies. He was paired with Rebecca Barnes for a project, and she was brilliant. She was one of the nicest girls he had ever met. He thought about her, and her long brown hair and golden brown eyes.

He'd traced over the heading of the paper with her name so often the paper had almost torn through. It didn't matter, Rebecca said she was going to type it up on the school computer. Still he didn't want her to see how he had messed up their notes.

A piece of pie was suddenly placed in front of him. He looked up and there was Margie. She owned the diner, and was like a second mother to his sister since theirs had died.

"Working hard I see."

"Huh?"

"Who's Rebecca Barnes?"

Billy put his hand over their names, and looked up at Margie.

"This is a project about Martin Luther King for social studies."

"Uh-huh. Not that he isn't a pretty interesting guy, but I don't think he has you mooning over him. Who's the girl? If you spill it to me I won't tell your sister." Margie sat down across from him.

"What girl?" Billy groaned as he looked up and saw Darius Stanton towering over the table. Darius was one of the Navy SEALs in Mason's unit. Mason was practically his big brother, so all of these guys considered him his little brother too.

"Nobody."

"Rebecca Barnes," Margie answered. "She's in his civics class."

"Social studies," Billy corrected.

"Order up," Peter yelled from the back.

"I guess my break is over." Margie got up from the booth. She fluffed Billy's hair, and he hunched over.

"I guess you're too old for that?"

"Yeah. But it makes her feel good so I don't want to hurt her feelings. It's not worth complaining about." Darius tilted his head and smiled.

"I knew I liked you."

"I thought it was because we both spent time in foster homes."

"Well there is that. Speaking of which, do you still talk to the Bards?" Darius asked, referring to the people Billy had lived with for over two years.

"Yeah, Mason, Sophia, and I were just over there for a barbeque two weeks ago. The twins are both in gymnastics. Do you stay in touch with the people you fostered with?"

"Only the last guy we stayed with, Old Henry, nobody else."

"Who's we?"

"The two other guys I was in foster care with, Donny and Steve. We were together for over ten years. Anyway, Old Henry took us in when we were about your age, he was great."

"Is he dead?"

"Nah, he actually wasn't that old. He was probably fifty, he just seemed old at the time. He was a retired sergeant from the Army. So who is Rebecca Barnes, and don't tell me she's nobody."

"We were paired to work on this project together. We're meeting at the library tomorrow." Billy toyed with the pie in front of him. "Dare, she's really quiet. I try to get her to talk. I know people pick on her." Immediately Darius was looking at him, really looking at him.

"Why?"

"She's a foster. She's in one of those homes, with three other kids, where they do it to collect the checks. She's always wearing Goodwill clothes. She thinks I'm just being nice to her. When I brought up I was in foster care too, she shut down."

Darius took a deep breath. "I know just the kind of places you're talking about."

"What do I do? What do I say?"

"I take it you want to be more than just a friend?"

It was Billy's turn to take a deep breath.

"I want to invite her to the Valentine's Day Dance, but even though some of the girls pick on her, the guys hit on her. She's turned down two of them already. Hell, Dare, maybe I ought to settle for what I've got and stay friends with her."

Darius just stared.

"Yeah, I want more. But I'm going to be fourteen next month, and she just had her birthday last month. It's not like we're going to get married. But I sure do think about kissing her. I think about it a lot."

"You're on the right track. The part where you need to start out as friends. Have you talked to Sophia?"

"I can't. She still sees me as her baby brother. She practically raised me. She can't see me as older."

"She will. She's just needs a little more time. Talk to Mason."

Billy thought about it. Maybe Dare was right, maybe he was doing this correctly. And talking to Mason was a brilliant idea.

Billy finally felt good enough to start eating pie.

CHAPTER TWO

Darius Stanton

Darius went outside to gently lean on his '67 Ford Mustang Convertible. It was his baby. She was powder blue, and the idea of getting a smudge on his car wasn't worth thinking about. He pulled out his phone and called one of his friends on speed dial.

"Gregory."

"What? You don't even have time to say 'hello' or your first name anymore?"

"Cut the shit, Dare. No, I don't." Steve sounded irritated.

"Are you okay?"

"No I'm not, what do you need?"

"How about a beer after work?"

"Can't. Work never ends." God, his friend sounded terrible.

"I'm picking you up at seven. You're leaving the office whether you want to or not."

"Seriously, Dare, I can't. I'm up to my ass in alligators. Do you know how overloaded the San Diego foster care system is? I can't find enough people to foster the kids, and it seems like every single one I do find is shit. I live, eat, and breathe this. I can't take any time off."

"Perfect, I want to talk about a case. The difference is you get to eat some dinner with an old friend and have a beer." He heard his friend thinking.

"One beer. You're buying. You pick me up." The phone went dead. Then it rang again.

"Stanton," Darius answered, just to get his friend's goat.

"I want gossip. You haven't been serial dating for

months now. I want to hear about the woman who has your tail tied in a knot." The phone went dead again.

Fuck.

* * *

"Okay, you were right. I needed to get away from the office."

"I'm always right." Darius grinned at Steve.

"Don't make me spit up a perfectly good beer."

"Hey have you seen Donny's infomercials?" Darius asked about their foster brother.

"I hear he barely skated by without being indicted the last time. Seriously, this is a Ponzi scheme."

"You're tuning him out when you watch those infomercials in the middle of the night, aren't you?" Darius asked. "This one he's not asking for investors. Instead you go to the hotel near the airport and pay to hear his investing ideas. You invest in his *expertise*. No Ponzi scheme. He's finally figured out how to sell his bullshit."

Steve stared with his mouth open in awe.

"You've got to be shitting me. People pay our Donny for advice?"

"I know, right?"

When Steve could finally talk again, he asked, "Tell me about the new case you're wanting me to investigate, and this woman in your life. Not in that order."

Darius rubbed the outside of his beer mug.

"You wouldn't believe the woman stuff."

"Try me."

"She's almost like a spy. She's this incredible hacker who robs drug lords to fund shelters. She scares the shit out of me. She's always in some fucking situation that could possibly get her killed."

"Oh shit, that's priceless. You're the straight arrow guy who wanted to be a doctor. You wouldn't cross the street against the light until you were thirteen. Even then Donny had to dare you."

"I've learned how to color outside the lines," Darius defended himself.

"Enough for a girl like this?"

"She doesn't need somebody who breaks the rules, she does enough of that on her own. She needs a bloody keeper."

"How long have you been dating?"

"Ha!" Darius' laugh was loud and bitter. "We've never dated. I've met her once, and talked to her a few times. I'm pretty sure she lives in Oklahoma. She faked her own death when she was seventeen to get out of an abusive foster home."

"Sounds to me like you have your work cut out for you SEAL-Boy."

"Would you not call me that?"

"If the flipper fits…"

Darius pulled a piece of paper from his pocket. "Here's the information on Rebecca Barnes. I think she's in a foster farm. She just turned fourteen. She's coping, but she shouldn't have to."

"Ah shit Darius, coping is better than having to live in a group home, which is what a lot of kids are dealing with."

They sat there silently and drank their beers.

"So how bad is it? I thought it was better than when we were in the system. You were going to clean it up, Steve."

"It's all about funding and finding people who will come forward to be foster parents. Good people."

"You got the Peppers shut down."

"Fuck that, yours and my testimony got the old man sent to jail." Steve raised his glass. Darius gave a half hearted smile. To this day, it seemed too little, too late.

"Yeah, but Mrs. Pepper would still be taking in kids if it hadn't been for you. Hell, her daughter started to foster, and you stopped her dead in her tracks." Darius raised his glass again.

"When was the last time you saw Old Henry?" Steve asked.

"Yesterday." Darius grinned. "He told me you were working too much and I needed to kidnap you. Said I was uniquely qualified for such a mission." Steve snorted.

"Let's order food or I'll never be able to get work done tonight. What else did Henry say?"

"That you, me, and even Donny were the best things that ever happened to him."

"Isn't that a hoot, since living with him was the best thing that ever happened to us," Steve murmured.

CHAPTER THREE

Mason Gault

Sophia traced the contours of Mason's chest with her fingers. Mason cherished his Sunday mornings with Sophia. She didn't have to be at the diner early so he got to watch the colors of dawn wash over her body and paint her skin with golden light.

On these mornings, without the alarm, she awoke like a kitten. All soft purrs, brushing against him, rolling and twisting until she found the right position for them to snuggle. Sophia had one leg draped over his hips, and he held her head nestled under his chin. His fingers sifted through the fine silk of her golden blonde hair.

"Mason," she whispered.

"Good morning, beautiful," he whispered the lyrics of the song.

Her fingers dug into his chest, and he ached with hunger.

"You make me feel beautiful." He looked into her green eyes.

"Then I'm doing my job." He swept in for a kiss, loving the taste of her happy smile. He licked, and she opened, he took his time with tender forays, so they could enjoy their precious extra time this morning.

Her hands kneaded his neck, then worked their way upwards until she was scraping his scalp with her nails. He almost yowled with pleasure. She grinned into their kiss, and he broke it off to look into her dancing eyes.

"You know what you're doing, don't you?"

"Hopefully driving you out of your mind," she teased.

He cupped her breast, brushed the tip with his thumb, and she arched up with a gasp. "Mason, it's too much."

"Fair's, fair." He trailed his tongue between her breasts, then blew on the wet path making her senses sing. Ever downwards he went, loving how her soft tummy seemed to thrum with excitement. Her fingers stroked his cheek, and he rubbed the beard roughed skin against her hipbone. She shuddered.

"Mason," she moaned, moving her body against his face so the sensations could intensify. He coasted his hands behind her, gently caressed the backs of her thighs, and then parted them.

"You're so gorgeous, I couldn't ask for a more responsive lover." He dipped his head and gave a soft lick. His woman was soon writhing and begging for more.

"Please, come to me. Be with me." He moved slowly upwards, and pressed inside her warm depths. Mason savored the carnal connection blended with the beauty of Sophia's embrace.

The bond between them in these moments was so intense, that he was never quite sure who pleasured who.

But as always they took flight together and landed softly in one another's arms.

* * *

"I'm thinking you get something extra special for breakfast after that," Sophia said. She gave him a long slow kiss.

"Yes, and I should be the one doing the cooking." He smiled down at her.

"You just did." Sophia giggled, as she pushed at him. Mason rolled over and watched as she made her way into the bathroom. He laid there and listened, the shower ran for a bit before he went in to start shaving.

"Mason?"

"Mmmm?" He loved watching her put on her lotion in the mornings.

"Have you noticed anything weird about Billy? He seems to be preoccupied."

"Haven't you asked him about it? I mean, you two talk about everything."

"I have. Either it's about Dad and he's protecting me, or it's a girl, and he doesn't feel comfortable talking about it to me."

Mason pulled the blade across his chin, and considered what she said.

"I'll take him out surfing and see if I can get him to talk. On one condition. You arrange to take some days off. You've been working too hard." He cut his glance sideways and saw her give him a frown.

"It's the thing with the gourmet shops. I'm so excited they want to carry our line of baked goods. Plus I don't like leaving Margie in a lurch."

"You're not. You've hired two new girls. The diner's fine. You can tell the gourmet shops they'll have to wait a couple of weeks until you hire additional help. Anyway, my Mom wants to come down and start planning the wedding with you. So you have to." He watched her light up. He loved that his two best girls got along so well.

"That's great. But you know I'm going to keep the wedding simple." He rolled his eyes, and rinsed off his razor. He went over and kissed her.

"Whatever makes you happy, makes me happy."

* * *

Billy Anderson

He loved the days when Mason took him surfing. They had to be the best thing about having left the Bard's and moving back in with his sister. He stopped short, his feet buried in the sand. Mason continued to run towards the surf. Billy couldn't believe that thought had actually entered his head.

Living with Sophia really was the dream come true, and Mason was the cherry on top. Billy remembered how it had been before Mason came into the picture.

Sophia had been working her ass off to scrape together enough money for a place big enough for them. And it needed to meet the approval of DHS so she could regain custody of him. Then Mason came in to their lives, and it made the day he could move out of the Bards and in with Sophia happen much sooner. When he thought about all Sophia sacrificed on his behalf, no matter what kind of emotional shit he put her through, he knew he was blessed.

"Hey Billy, you afraid of sharks?" Mason yelled.

"They eat SEALs," Billy quipped. Mason laughed.

Billy trotted towards the water, and eyed the man who was going to marry his sister, and thought here was another blessing. He knew thinking in terms of blessings wasn't typical for a fourteen year old boy, but it was for one who watched his dad desert his family. It was for one who watched his mother waste away from cancer. It was for one who lived on the streets at times. Billy had vowed never to take his good fortune for granted. Which was why he refused to take Rebecca for granted.

"Billy, you listening to me?"

"Huh?"

"That's what I thought. Let's just sit and enjoy the sunrise, the waves will still be there. You can tell me what's on your mind if you want. You know I won't judge or tell anyone you don't want me to tell."

"Even Sophia?"

"Well it depends. If it concerns your health or safety, then yeah, I have to tell her., your safety comes first. If it is just something you need to confide in me, than no."

Billy considered what he said. He looked at Mason, and knew he could trust him. He realized it was probably why he made it to lieutenant in the SEAL team, he had good judgement and people could rely on him.

"It's about a girl. Her name is Rebecca Barnes. She's my partner on a social studies project." Billy rubbed the back of his neck, and then he gave a self-conscious laugh. He never used to do that, but it was exactly what Mason did when he was stressed.

"Tell me about her."

"She's nice to everyone even when they aren't nice to her. Too nice. I can't figure out if it's because she wants people to like her, or if she's wired that way. She needs to push back. But I think the fight's been beaten out of her. I'm worried that might of literally happened, and it's why she landed in foster care."

Billy stared off into the ocean. He'd thought about Rebecca for a long time. She reminded him of the abused golden retriever Lori Bard had brought home. Goldie had always flinched when someone raised their hand too fast, thinking they were going to hit her instead of pet her. At the same time she craved attention.

"You worry about her."

"I do. But she has great instincts." Billy grinned. He fished around in the sand and pulled out a stick.

"Tell me," Mason prompted.

"She's been asked out to the Valentine's Day Dance by two of the worst players at school. I mean they're slick. A lot of girls really want to go with them, and she turned them down flat. It was a thing of beauty."

Billy paused, and started digging in the sand with the stick.

"What?" Mason prompted.

"Actually the way she'd looked Eric from the top of his head to the tips of his toes and said, 'No thank you,' like he'd been something she needed to wipe off her shoe had been a little scary."

"You saw this happen, huh?"

"Yeah, he came up to her in the library where we were studying. After he left she explained his reputation was known far and wide. Apparently, he had started a nasty rumor about one girl after they'd gone out. Then with another girl he had pushed too hard for intimacy and left her in tears."

"Is this Eric Jameson?"

Shit, he was in for it now.

"Yeah, it's the same guy I had the unnecessary roughness foul with two weeks ago, when I got thrown out of the Lacrosse game." Billy looked sideways at Mason, but the man's expression didn't change.

"So you did it on purpose?"

"Yes."

"Would you do it again?"

"Yes.

"Are you going to do it again?"

"I won't have to. I got my point across. He knows why it happened, and what will happen in the future if he doesn't shape up."

"Okay then. So back to Rebecca. It sounds like, despite everything, she can handle herself."

"Maybe a little too well," Billy mumbled.

Mason chuckled. "So you want to ask her out, but you're afraid of getting wiped off her shoe."

"Something like that." Billy dug deeper into the sand, then finally threw the stick towards the ocean.

"Would it help to know that no matter how old you are, and how many times you've asked for dates, you always worry about that?"

"Did you worry about it with my sister?"

"I kind of side-stepped the asking out part. She needed a ride to her car, so I just arranged to pick her up from the hospital. I kind of kept maneuvering things until she got used to me. Seems to me like you have the same opportunity with the homework project."

Billy grinned. "Trust me, I've never needed as much tutoring as I have had with this project."

"Good man." Mason grinned in return. "So do you think she likes you?"

"Definitely as a friend. But I still don't know how she would feel about going out with me."

"Hmmm. Does she want to go to the dance?"

"I honestly don't know."

"I think you need to find out. Because if she does, going with a 'friend' would be pretty appealing."

Billy sighed.

"I know, it will still suck if she shoots you down." Mason bumped his shoulder with his.

"I can only tell you, if she does, there will be pizza and video games waiting for you at home. I'll even let you win."

"Hell, Mase, you never *let* me win. You're old, you naturally lose."

"In that case we're playing *Call of Duty*. You will lose on that one my man. I live that game." Billy laughed. It was true, Mason always beat him at *Call of Duty*.

Chapter Four

Finn Crandall

"Come on Mom, you have to admit it's better living here than in Minnesota." He grinned at the beautiful Scandinavian woman who was his mother.

"I don't have to do any such thing, Finnius."

Damn, apparently he was not scoring points if she was calling him Finnius. They were currently having lunch overlooking the Pacific Ocean. It was the end of January, and it was a beautiful sunny day.

He raised his eyebrow.

"I hated moving here and then having you gone for the first two months."

"I hated it too, Mom."

"Of course, you did arrange for Darius to babysit me. That was nice. You have nice friends. I've always liked your team mates."

"Is it the only thing you've liked about moving here? Being close to me and my friends?" he asked.

"Fine, it is a little bit better than being buried in three feet of snow," she admitted reluctantly.

"Was that so hard?"

"Yes," she said sadly. "I left your dad and my dad there."

Finn reached over and grasped his mother's hand, and she grabbed on tightly, tears in her eyes.

"We'll be visiting Gramps next month," he promised.

"Oh Finn, I don't want you wasting your leave on that. It's not like he knows who either of us are." She sounded so forlorn. He rubbed his thumb over the back of her hand.

"He does on some level, Mom."

"No, he doesn't. I've talked to the nurses. He's deteriorated to the point that he doesn't recognize anyone or anything."

Finn's heart clenched as he thought of his once vibrant grandfather. "Even more reason to go and visit."

She gave him a watery smile. "Thanks, son."

"And we'll go visit Dad's grave. Brush off the snow." He grinned. "Of course, *he* liked the snow," Finn teased.

"I remember you two going ice fishing, and him coaching your lacrosse team. I'm so happy you're taking the time to coach lacrosse."

"I never know what my schedule is like so I just run some clinics now and again, and ref when they ask me too."

"You're going to make a good father one day." Finn carefully schooled his features, but his mother wasn't fooled.

"You will, and you'll find the right girl. Look at Mason. Look at Clint."

"I'm not the same as Mason and Clint."

"No, you're better." Finn threw back his head and laughed, causing the seagulls to fly away from their perch on the deck posts.

"You know, since that girl in college you have given up all hope of a happily ever after." His mother leaned forward. "Ginger wasn't worthy of shining your shoes, let alone shining anything else of yours."

Sweet tea spewed out of his mouth, as he looked at Evie goggle-eyed.

"Good, I have your attention. Yes Finn, you were very focused in college. Yes, you're very focused and committed to your career now. Well welcome to the world. So are a lot of people, and they juggle relationships and family just fine. You will too son. So you better start looking around, because I want grandbabies."

His mother's words were reverberating throughout his head. She had not just said what he thought she had.

"Finn, are you hearing me?"

"Yes, Mom."

"Good, because I want to talk to you about your lack of dates."

"I go out on plenty of dates."

"I'm talking about women you respect and would consider a relationship with."

Fuck! Time to redirect.

"If you want to talk about dating, I could really use your help.

"Hallelujah. I thought you would never ask. Shoot." His mom propped her chin on her hand, and looked at him with avid interest.

"You remember Billy, Sophia's younger brother? Well, Mase wants me to watch out for him in the upcoming game because he's worried there might be some retaliation over an unnecessary roughness foul he did on a kid."

"Didn't I meet Billy at Clint and Lydia's engagement party? He doesn't strike me as the overly aggressive type of teenage boy."

Score one for team redirect!

"He's not, apparently the other kid was an asshole, and had hurt one or two girls at school. Billy was making a point. Mase didn't think Billy would do anything again, but he wanted me to keep an eye out for any retaliation."

"What does that have to do with dating?"

"Mase told me this in confidence, so I'd understand the whole situation. Billy found out about this kid's behavior from a girl Eric had asked out. This girl is a friend of Billy's, and Billy wants to ask her out. Mason thinks Eric will realize how close Billy and the girl are, and will *really* be gunning for Billy."

"So tell me about the girl."

"Mase didn't give me a lot of details. Like I said, it was in confidence, and wasn't the real point of the story. Hell, even if he did, I wouldn't remember much about a fourteen year old girl. To tell you the truth, I can't even remember the first girl I asked for a date."

"That's because you never did ask one out. They started calling you in sixth grade and never stopped.

That's why Ginger did such a number on you. Don't you remember the seventh grade dance? Your problem was three girls kept calling the house, and you kept begging your dad and me not to answer the phone?"

Finn thought back to Laurie. She'd been the one who had basically bullied him into going, and he had really wanted to go with Zoe. It wasn't until he had been in ninth grade that he had learned how to say no to the girls he didn't want to date.

"I sure did have it easy when it came to girls."

"Yes you did," his mom agreed. "But is it always easy for you now?"

Finn stopped himself from immediately saying yes. Hell, it was easy, but it was because it hadn't mattered. Evie eyed him.

Damn, they were getting into dangerous waters. Time to redirect...again.

Finn looked down at his watch and swore.

He signaled to the waiter for the bill.

"Don't worry, I've got lunch today. You can pay next time." His mother assured him.

"Okay, I love you, Mom," he said as he got up to leave. As he passed the waiter, he handed him three bills. His mom shook her head in exasperation and laughed. He waved good-bye.

Finn made good time to the field. He'd thought ahead and had most of the equipment in his old 1972 El Camino. When he got there, a group of parents nodded in his direction, and toasted him with their coffee cups. He didn't have to say a thing to the boys, they were already scrambling away from the field to his car. Billy was one of the first three boys to arrive.

"Can you men help get the equipment over to the field?" he asked.

A bunch of affirmatives were matched with hands reaching to take the sticks and bags.

Finn reached into the front seat and pulled out his roster. There were supposed to be five boys at the goalie clinic. So far there were only four.

"Hey Billy, I recognize you, Stan and Michael. Is the other kid over there Hal or Luke?"

"He's Hal." Finn looked at his watch. They weren't due to start for another five minutes. He'd give the other kid 'til five after, then he'd start whether he showed or not.

"So did they pull you out for just the one game, or are you out for multiple games?" Finn asked.

"Mason talked to you, huh?"

"Yeah. Nothing bad. It sounded like the kid probably deserved it. Still if you pull that shit on the field somebody else could end up with a stick in the face. You've got to be careful." Finn watched Billy, and the boy didn't flinch.

"I was careful. Nobody else was in the area. I wanted to make sure it just impacted Eric, the last thing I wanted was an innocent to get harmed."

Fuck, it was like listening to Mason, Finn thought to himself.

"So this kid had it coming?"

"He ruined one girl's reputation, and pushed another too far. Yeah, he deserved it. He knows I'll be keeping an eye on him."

"Just like I'm going to have an eye on you. This kid sounds like the type who'd pull in others and come after you on the field. That's why Mase asked me to keep an eye out, so I will."

"I suppose something like that is always possible, he's a bully. I think he's just going to lick his wounds and re-member my warning."

Yep, he definitely sounded like Mason.

"Did he mess with a girl who's important to you?"

Finn watched as Billy's fists clenched.

"Nope." It made Finn wonder what would have hap-pened if he had.

Finn smiled. "So there's a girl?"

"Yeah." Billy sighed. "There is. She's pretty great."

"And this guy didn't do anything inappropriate with her?"

"No, he didn't say or do anything to Rebecca. She was the one who told me when he asked her out. He asked her the day before I was going to." Billy looked across the field at the other players."

"Then you got worried about her turning you down too, right?"

"You got it."

Finn nodded.

"I shouldn't have waited. I should have asked her out then and there. But the more I let it slide the worse it gets, ya know?"

"I hear that."

"I should never have procrastinated," Billy said with disgust.

"I don't know, at least you're putting together a game plan," Finn said as he hefted a bag of equipment and started walking towards the field. "I think going in with a plan always beats bursting in and not knowing what to expect."

"I guess."

"Plus, you've probably laid some groundwork." Billy perked up.

"It's kind of like this, you're hitting your fundamentals, you're practicing, and you're building your foundation."

"A sports analogy, Finn?" Billy shook his head with a grin.

"I'm a firm believer in sports teaching you a lot of good things for life. You my boy have probably built a foundation of trust, am I right?" Billy laughed.

"Yes."

"Build on that, and you'll be going to the dance." They looked up as another car pulled up and a new boy got out.

"Looks like the clinic can start now," Finn said.

CHAPTER FIVE

Clint Archer

"Billy, for the last time. We wanted you to come with us," Lydia said as she shelled out for the massive amounts of popcorn, soda, pretzels, and candy.

"Kid, you ask again I'll be forced to kill you," Clint growled good naturedly.

"It just seemed too perfect. I love Mason's mom, but I really didn't want to have to stay at the house and listen to them talk about wedding stuff. I was really impressed Mase was willing to stick around and talk about flowers and what color the tablecloths should be."

"It's important to your sister," Clint said.

"I know, but still." He made a face, then bounded ahead of them towards the theater. Clint smiled to himself when he realized how much food he was carrying. His smile extended to Lydia as they followed at a slightly more leisurely pace, but his woman was as excited as Billy to get to her seat. She wasn't fooling him, she didn't want to miss one single preview.

"Speed it up, SEAL-Boy. I can't believe you're moving so slow."

"It's because you have me loaded down with enough junk food to feed a small nation."

"Oh, quit your bitching, you know you're going to eat most of mine anyway." She was right, but still, how in the hell they could drop more money on food at the theater than they could at an expensive dinner was beyond him.

They were the second set of people in the theaters, so Lydia was still using her outside voice.

"Billy, you're not a talker at the movies, are you?" It was clear his answer had to be no, and the kid was not stupid.

"No, ma'am."

"Cut the crap, you know my name is Lydia."

"No Lydia, I'm not a talker during the movie." Billy grinned. Like Clint thought, the kid wasn't stupid.

"Okay, Clint's in the middle so he can hold my food, and I can be free to enjoy the movie. Now it's okay to talk during the previews. After all we need to give them the thumbs up or thumbs down. So commentary is practically mandatory."

They were at the theater with the reclining seats, so Clint watched in fascination as Lydia played around with hers until she had just the setting she wanted. God, he loved this woman. He loved it when she was so excited she was bursting at the seams with orders, especially when he knew tonight he would be taking over and she would enjoy every moment of him *giving* the orders.

All three of them agreed on the new James Bond movie.

He was voted against on a new movie with Tom Cruise. How could they take him seriously as a military man?

It went on and on, and finally the lights were going down. Lydia leaned over his lap, and whispered to Billy.

"The one exception to the no talking rule is, 'he who spots Stan Lee first, gets major points'."

"Gotchya."

* * *

Clint totally approved of how Billy wanted to spend his 'major points'.

"I'm so excited Beth and Jack are going to meet us here," Lydia enthused.

"I haven't met, Beth. She wasn't at your engagement party," Billy said.

"Do me a favor kid and never mention that again. As a matter of fact, I'll pay for extra laps around the track, if you don't even bring up the fact Lydia and I are engaged in front of Lydia's sister."

Clint pulled his souped-up truck into the K-1 Indoor Racing Center parking lot.

"You got it, Clint," Billy agreed.

"I see Jack's car." Lydia pointed to a decked out SUV. "They must already be inside."

Clint let her out at the entrance, while he and Billy went to park the truck.

"So what's the deal? Why wasn't Beth at the big surprise engagement party you threw for Lydia?"

"I fucked up. It's a long story. There was a piece of shit out after Beth, and I thought I was protecting her. She still doesn't much talk to me. All I can say, is at least she isn't a lot like Lydia, otherwise I'd have to sleep with one eye open."

Billy nodded. They opened the door to the center, and were met with a draft of cool air, and the scent of gasoline. Clint went to pay for the tickets, but was met by a big blonde man.

"Clint, it's already covered. Thanks for inviting us. This sounds like a blast."

"Hi, Jack. You didn't have to pay."

"I know." Jack tipped his chin towards the two women who were chatting away while trying to get helmets. "I love the idea of Beth trying this out."

"She's become quite the surprise," Clint agreed. "She'll probably kick all of our asses."

"Nope, I'm the one who's going to do that," Billy piped up.

"Hi. I'm Jack Preston. You must be Billy Gault." Jack held out his hand.

"Billy Anderson," Billy corrected. "I'm Mason's soon-to-be brother-in-law. Clint and Lydia have rescued me from the horror of wedding planning."

The blonde giant grinned. "Clint's a good man."

Clint watched as Billy took out his phone, and frowned. Then he carefully keyed in a response. He waited, and then smiled.

"Everything okay?"

"Yeah, I'm just scheduling my next study session on Martin Luther King, Jr. with my social studies partner."

Jack gave him a sideways glance. Then they both looked at Billy.

"That sure was a lot of concentration on a text for just a study session, Billy," Clint said. "Is your study partner a girl?"

Billy shook his head resignedly. "I'm that obvious?"

"Only to another man."

"Hey," Lydia interrupted. "They don't have a helmet that fits Beth. We're going to go talk to the people up front."

"Beth, show me the one they end up giving you, okay?" Jack said to the woman who looked so much like Lydia. Her eyes shined bright as she nodded.

"We're also going to go look around. They said it would take a half hour before we would get to race. I want to watch some of the other people do their laps," Beth said.

"We'll be over there," Clint said pointing to some tables near the food stalls.

"Okay." Clint watched as Jack brushed a kiss on Beth's lips. He loved seeing how tender the big man was with Beth. She might have come out of her shell with a bang, but in Clint's opinion she would always need that kind of loving care.

As the two women walked away, he admired Lydia's ass. Now his woman, his woman was almost one hundred percent fire. There were those rare moments she too needed to be cossetted. He loved being the man who could put out the fire, and also cherish her when she needed it. He was a hell of a lucky man.

"Give it up, Billy, he's admiring Lydia's attributes," Jack said.

Clint turned and saw Jack and Billy laughing at him. He scowled.

"What?"

"We wondered if you wanted to order food."

"Fuck no, we ate half the menu at the theater. We'll eat after the races." He walked towards the table. Billy and Jack were still laughing. He found it funny too, but he couldn't let *them* know.

They all sat down, and both men turned towards Billy.

"Your turn, spill it," Clint said.

"I liked laughing at you better." Billy laughed at him. Clint really liked Billy Anderson. Sophia and Mason had done a great job instilling confidence in him. Considering he had been in foster care two years ago, and now he was giving shit to two Navy SEALs, it was pretty damned amazing.

"I'm sure you do like laughing at me better. But I already *have* my woman. Seems to me like you *don't* have yours. Let's see if Jack and I can give you some advice."

"You can't. I just have to man up," Billy said dejectedly.

"What do you mean?" Jack asked.

"Rebecca Barnes is my social studies partner. I want to ask her to the Valentine's Day Dance. I'm nervous about asking her out, but I just have to man up and do it."

Clint shared a pointed look with Jack.

"You know that half the asking is really up to her, don't you?" Jack asked.

"Huh?"

"What Jack means is she puts out signals as to whether she likes you and whether she wants to be asked."

"She does?" Clint looked at the boy who was soon going to be a man. He was now at the gangly stage where his feet and hands were too big for his body. He looked almost like a puppy as he glanced from him to Jack and back to him again.

"Yep. Women and girls have been leading us around for years." Clint chuckled. "At least it's what my sister Jenny told me when I was fourteen."

"I still don't get it."

"Billy, how comfortable do you feel around Rebecca?" Jack asked.

"I've never felt so good around a girl. She makes me feel smart. When we're together, she acts like I'm her best friend even though I know Cammie is."

"That means she really likes you," Clint piped up. Billy rolled his eyes.

"Clint, I know that. She likes me as a *friend*."

"No girl makes a guy, a teenage guy, feel that good unless she likes, and I mean really, *likes* him," Jack said.

"But what about you? Do you really like her? Is this her first dance? Because this shit is important. I remember when somebody was an asshole to my little sister." Clint gave Billy a hard stare.

"Damn, Clint, the kid wouldn't be this tied up in knots if she didn't really matter to him," Jack said.

Clint smiled. "Sorry Billy, just had a flashback to my sister crying. Seriously dude, she's sending out the right signals. She *likes* you, likes you. Go forth and ask her out." Clint cocked his head. "I just heard our names called."

* * *

"Were you giving Billy dating advice," Lydia asked later that night.

Clint traced the soothing lotion onto Lydia's back, paying special attention to the three raised scars.

"Yes."

"Do you wish somebody had given you advice when you were growing up?" she asked as she arched into his touch. Clint loved the fact she now relished his hands on this part of her body she once tried to hide from him.

"No, I like who I turned out to be. If I had been more social, I don't know if I would have gotten my mad computer skills and ended up being your Dork King." Lydia giggled, and he peeked over her shoulder so he could see her breasts bounce.

"I can tell your ogling my breasts," she whispered.

"I'd have to be dead for three years before I stop ogling your breasts, Ms. Hildalgo." He poured more of the luscious smelling lotion into his hands, and then smoothed around her ribcage and cupped her generous flesh. She let out a moan of pleasure.

"I think tonight I want you to let me have my way with you, what do you think of that?"

"I think since I end up with three hundred million orgasms that way, I'm all for it."

He kissed the shell of her ear.

"Lie down on the bed, baby." She shifted from a sitting position, and was soon lying in front of him like a succulent playground. The mind boggled, his eyes kept shifting unable to figure out where to look.

"Clint, please touch me." Lydia lifted her arms. He linked their fingers and eased over her, then brought her arms outward until they were spread wide. He let go.

"Keep them there, baby. I don't want any interruptions while I play." She whimpered, but nodded.

"Good girl."

He scanned her again, and took in the visual feast she presented. Her breasts jutted up, her rose brown nipples against her golden skin were too much to resist. He swooped down and started to suckle.

"More. Harder." He kept going, his fingers plucking at her other nipple, continuing until her hands clutched his head.

Bingo.

"Lydia, where do your hands belong?"

"Dammit," she whined, but eventually she put them back.

He laughed at her slow progress. He lowered his head and rewarded them both.

"Please, Clint, you promised me orgasms," she panted out.

He trailed his hand lower, and she parted her thighs in welcome. She was so ready, so needy, so wonderfully wet. He found her engorged flesh, and played in time to the licks on her nipple. She let out a wail of completion that shot satisfaction to his soul.

This time, when her hands moved and she grabbed his ass, he didn't care.

"I'm claiming my orgasm the way I really want it. With you inside me." Who was he to disagree?

With shallow thrusts he tested her, and she whined in frustration.

"Stop teasing!"

He smiled. Teasing Lydia was a joy.

She pushed upwards, and he retreated. She growled, and he laughed.

"Clint! You're killing me."

"Put your hands over your head." Her eyes heated up, and her body clenched around him. He wasn't going to last.

Finally she released him, and complied, which arched her torso like a beautiful temptation. He pulled her tight against him, and started a strong rhythm. She let out a happy laugh.

Clint kissed her smiling lips, and she took a nip at his. They played and loved, as she pressed up, and he thrust down.

"So good, you're so damn good at this."

"It's you, Lydia, it's always been you, love." She wrapped her legs around him, and demanded more, which he gladly gave. And once again, she proved to him it *was* her as she took him on a tour of the stars.

CHAPTER SIX

Jack Preston

"Hop on in."

"Don't you think I should be driving since I beat you yesterday?" Billy teased. Jack liked the kid even more for the smart ass comment.

"Tell you what, you can definitely practice in my car when you get your learner's permit."

"Really?" Jack pulled onto the Five Freeway heading north to San Clemente.

"Really. But no lapping the other cars like you did yesterday. I don't want you to get pulled over and have your learner's permit pulled the first day out."

"Jack, why are you willing to come out to the Food Pantry so early in the morning on a Sunday?"

He loved kids, they asked what was on their minds.

"My mom and I lived in a women's shelter when I was little, I always try to give back when I have time. Sophia told me about this place, and it sounded like a great place to volunteer. Frannie and Tony said this is when they get deliveries and needed the most help sorting the food."

"I know, it's why I come on these days. Usually Mason or Sophia drop me off." Billy yawned. "But Sundays are Sophia's one day to sleep in, so it was great when you said you could pick me up. Thanks."

"No problem." They stayed silent for a while. Both admiring the view of the sun glimmering on the Pacific Ocean.

"Take a left here, and then the first right," Billy directed.

A truck was already at the back, and a man who had left middle age behind, was helping the deliveryman unload the truck. Jack eyed the dolly he was maneuvering, and guessed it to have at least two hundred pounds of boxes. He stopped the car quickly and got out. Billy followed at a fast clip.

"Hey Mr. D," Billy called out. "I brought reinforcements. He's the brawn, and I'm the brains," Billy quipped. "Mrs. D, your big new recruit is here, and Mr. D. is trying to get another hernia," Billy yelled into the back door of the building.

"Billy, I can't believe you would tell on me like that. For shame."

"Tony, stop with the dolly this instant," Frannie DeLuca said as she came outside, the early morning light causing her flaming red hair to glow.

"I'm fine. I have it all under control," he grunted.

"Let the young guns do the heavy lifting," she had the raspy voice of a former smoker, and the loving tone of a wife who adored her husband.

"I know exactly where this needs to go," Tony protested.

"And you can supervise, when Jack takes it there. I'm assuming you're Jack, right?"

"Yes, ma'am. I'm great at taking direction."

"Good to know. I'm great at bossing good looking men around." She winked at him. "Isn't that right Billy?" She put her arm around the young man and headed him into the building.

"I'm happy to have you lift and carry. But tell Frannie I made a big deal about protesting. I like her to think I'm still a stud, okay?" Jack laughed.

"You got it, Mr. D." He followed the man in, maneuvering the dolly. They made quick work of unloading all of the food onto the appropriate shelves. Next came the pallets of fruit. Tony looked at them in disgust.

"Seriously, they send more of this crap every week."

"What?" Jack asked as they unloaded crate after crate of bananas.

"Rotten fruit. There is no way we can set out this stuff for the people. I'd say more than two thirds will have to be thrown out. They're using us for a tax write off."

"Tony, don't get so upset, remember your blood pressure." Tony pulled over a large green trash can, and sorted through the produce.

"To hell with my blood pressure." Tony threw the fruit forcefully into the can, and Billy winced. He looked at Jack.

"Hey Mr. D, I meant to ask you something," he whispered, after Frannie walked away muttering about stubborn men.

"What is it kid?" He threw two bunches of bananas into the container.

"Jack was telling me girls gave off signals if they liked you. Is that true?" Tony paused with the next batch in his hands, looked over at Jack, and then back at Billy.

"You like some girl? A lot?"

"I want to ask her out."

"That's a lot," Tony said, as he sat down on one of the pallets, the rotten fruit forgotten. "So Mr. Navy SEAL, what was your advice?"

"I had some generic advice, but I really need to know more about the girl."

"She's been hurt I think. She's in foster care. I think she's been abandoned, but she hasn't told me. Sometimes I see she's really sad."

"That's a special kind of girl, who will probably need to be treated delicately."

"I don't understand."

"Yes you do," Tony interrupted. "Think of your sister after those thugs hurt her. Mason had to be very cautious with her."

"He did?"

"Ah damn kid, you were still with the Bards, weren't you?" Tony remembered.

"My fiancé, Beth, had been hurt, and she needed to know she was safe. I didn't have to do anything I didn't want to do, so it was no hardship. But, I did have to make sure she knew she was valued and cared for more often than I would have with a woman who hadn't been hurt. Does that make sense?"

Jack saw Billy's perplexed look.

"I needed to give her more outward signs of affection and care, I couldn't assume she knew what I was thinking and feeling, even when it made me more vulnerable."

"Oh." Billy nodded. Then he grimaced. "That must have been kind of hard."

"Not when you really care. I loved Beth. I'd have done anything for her." Jack thought back to those early days with her, and he couldn't help but smile.

CHAPTER SEVEN

Drake Avery

It had taken Drake two days to find the perfect opening. He knew Mason would often pick up Billy after school and drive him to his sister's diner to do his homework. Then she would drive him back home at night. This just required a little bit of planning. Step one was arranging it so his lieutenant had to stay late at work, which he had done.

"Mason, bummer about you having to redo the training manual. I don't know how it could have gotten corrupted." Mason looked up from the computer and gave Drake a hard look.

"Yeah, pretty weird."

"Good news is I can go pick up Billy from school and drop him off with Sophia." Mason's frown cleared.

"Thanks, I was worried about that."

"Not a problem. What are friends for?" Drake whistled to himself as he left the annex building.

Drake parked his truck across the street from the school, got out, and waited. He watched as Billy exited the school. Billy was with a girl, and he scanned the area. Drake liked the way the kid was aware of his surroundings. The girl was looking around like she was expecting a ride. Billy handed her his cell phone, and he could see how she reluctantly took it but finally made a call. It was obvious she got voicemail. She straightened her shoulders, gave Billy a fake smile, and started to walk away. Billy easily caught up and started to walk backwards in front of her, trying to convince her of something. Probably trying to get her to take a ride home. It looked like it was time for Uncle Drake to step in. He meandered over to the pair.

"Hey Billy." Billy looked over, unsurprised to see him.

"Hey Drake, this is Rebecca. Rebecca, this is my friend Drake, he works with my brother." Rebecca's eyes got wide as she took in the width and breadth of him.

"You're a soldier like Mason?" she asked quietly.

"A SEAL." He held out his hand, and she placed her hand in his. He shook it gently. He saw Billy's look of approval, and it made him feel good.

My how times were 'a changing'.

"Do you need a ride, Rebecca? I have my truck right over there. I was going to take Billy to his sister's for a piece of pie, and so he could start on his homework. Of course the pie is the most important part of the scenario."

She gave a soft laugh. It was a pretty sound.

"It's okay, I can walk home."

"Rebecca, it's five miles," Billy protested.

"It's not the first time."

"I know, but it's the first time I know about it ahead of time and can do something about it. Let Drake drive you. He's trustworthy, I promise."

Rebecca gave a quick look down to her shoes, if he hadn't been concentrating on her so hard, Drake might have missed it. They didn't fit right. They were too small. Dammit, they'd hurt walking all that way.

"Rebecca, I can't have you walking all that way alone on my watch. It's not allowed in the code book," Drake said with a straight face.

"Code book?"

"Yep, there's a code book SEALs have to live by, and leaving women and children in bad situations is not allowed. Seriously, I would have to turn myself in to my lieutenant for bad conduct if I didn't take care of you."

"You can't possibly be serious?" She looked over at Billy for validation.

"My brother Mason is his lieutenant. He'd be upset. Look, it'd be the same thing if Mase were here. You should hear how he met my sister. He was living by the same code. It's hard-wired."

She still didn't look convinced, but she grinned, but then it was wiped clean by a sad look.

"Rebecca, are you okay?"

"It's just when they don't answer they usually aren't there, and I don't have a key, but it's okay, the porch is covered and has a really comfy chair to sit on."

Oh hell no!

"Well do you have homework?"

She nodded.

"Do you like pie?

She nodded.

"I'm taking you and Billy to the diner."

"They'll be upset if I'm not there waiting for them when they get home."

Upset, not worried.

"Fuck 'em. Get in the truck. I'll talk to them when I drive you home," Drake assured her. He ushered her in front of him towards the truck, and Billy gave him the thumbs up sign.

When they got to the diner, there was a booth set aside for Billy. Sophia was busy with customers, so she didn't have a chance to come over and ask questions.

"Hi kids. Drake." Margie handed them menus.

"Rebecca this is Margie, she owns the diner."

"Sophia is busy, and she might have to leave for a bit. I'm going to be taking care of you. Figure out what you want, and I'll come back and take your orders." Drake opened his mouth to say something.

"Avery, if you make one move towards your wallet, we're going to have an issue. Am I clear?"

Drake laughed. "We're clear." Margie moved to the next table to take an order.

Rebecca asked where the restroom was, so Drake and Billy had a couple of minutes alone.

"Okay, so what's the scoopage? And give it to me fast kid."

"What do you mean?"

"Why do her parents suck? Why are you having a hard time asking her to the dance when she's a fucking doll? Why don't her clothes fit? When did you grow up to be such a man? Those things."

"She's a foster kid, and the foster family only cares about the money they get from the state. They obviously don't spend it on Rebecca. I already told Darius, he's checking into it. I'm scared to ask her out, even though I really like her, because she's turned down two other guys. And what do you mean I've grown up?"

"I'm going to help Dare to get her the fuck out of that fucking worthless house. You're a man, because of how you treat her. I respect you Billy. You're someone who I would want to serve with in a few years, and that's fucking saying something. As for asking her out? Just fucking do it. I doubt you'll get shot down, but if you do, keep her as a friend. She's going to be worth the long haul. You can tell. She's coming back." Drake got out of the booth.

"Rebecca, I've got a couple of errands to run, I'll be back in two hours to take you and Billy home. It was nice meeting you. Be kind to my friend here, he's a good man." Billy glared at him.

He could see Sophia motioning for him to come to the kitchen, so he went.

"Mason called, he said for you to check your voice-mail, Drake." He didn't need to, he'd seen the missed calls. Mase must have figured out he'd been the one to dink with the training manuals.

"Anyway, thanks for driving Billy. Is that Rebecca?" Sophia asked as she peeked around him to get a better look at the girl.

"Yep."

"How'd Billy talk her into coming here to study?"

"It's a long story. Look, I have to go. I promised her pie, so you can go introduce yourself." He watched Sophia grin. God, he liked Mason's woman, she was such a sweetie.

"I'll be back in two hours to take them home."

"Are you sure?" Sophia took off her apron and put it up on a hook. "I have to meet with some folks at a gourmet shop who want to order some of my pies. I was going to come back to drive him home after I was done." Sophia told him.

"Nope, I've already promised. Don't want to break my promise to the girl after just meeting her." Drake looked around the diner kitchen and saw what he wanted. "I'm going to see Frannie and Tony, can I get some cinnamon rolls to go?" He almost drooled as he watched Sophia drizzle on the icing. She closed the plastic container, and also put some muffins into a bag.

"What are these for?"

"They're orange cranberry muffins especially made for Tony." Drake looked into the bag with interest.

"They're low carb and low fat. Hopefully he'll eat these for a few days to make up for today's cinnamon rolls."

"Gotchya." Drake grabbed his bounty and headed for the front of the diner, as Sophia grabbed her coat and left out the back of the diner.

"See you guys in two hours." He waved to the kids.

He drove down the couple of blocks to the food bank and parked the car. He pulled out his cell and dialed Darius.

"Dare, you know about this problem with Billy's girl, right?" he demanded as soon as Darius answered. Drake was met by silence which made him crazy.

"Goddamit, answer me."

"Billy who?"

"Don't fuck with me, Stanton. I know where you live."

"Who clued you in on Billy's love life?"

"I overheard Clint and Jack talking about it. I figured he could probably use my perspective as well. Hell, I'm the one with sisters coming out the wazoo."

"If Mason wanted you to know about it, he would have told you, don't you think?"

"Mason doesn't have the sense God gave an ant. He doesn't realize what a great resource I truly am. Luckily I was able to get some time alone with the kid, and meet Rebecca. She's a doll. Billy has chosen well."

"So what does this have to do with me, except to make me an accessory after the fact?" Darius asked.

"The foster home where she is at is neglecting her. They didn't arrange a ride to pick her up from school. Her shoes are too small to walk home. Then she told us when she was going to get home, nobody would be there, and she doesn't have a key to get in."

"Ah shit. I was afraid of something like that."

"So you're already on the case? If you are, what the fuck is taking so long? Shit man, this is neglect! Don't you have friends in the San Diego Foster Care system?"

"Yes."

"Then make this shit right!"

"It's not that easy."

"Make it that easy."

"Fuck you, Avery!" Darius shouted.

"For real? We can't get her yanked?" Drake felt the wind get knocked out of his sails. He'd been counting on Darius.

"Are you telling me in your world there have been unicorns plopping out ice cream turds, and belching out cotton candy?" Darius asked in a resigned voice.

"In the world I grew up in there weren't such things as unicorns or rainbows. I was just hoping you might know of one. I'm sorry, Dare. I can't stand seeing another little girl suffer. I can't. We have to do something."

"And we will, Drake, I promise." Drake felt some of the tension drain from his chest.

"Do you want to come to San Clemente and meet her? She's here at the diner."

"I'm in the middle of something. I can't." Drake heard a note of frustrated pain in his friend's voice.

"It's Rylie, isn't it? You're trying to track her down. Look, I'll help you after this settles."

"Don't think I won't be working on this thing with Rebecca, because I am on it. I just can't afford to come up to San Clemente at the moment. I'm running down a lead."

"Understood. Good luck." Drake hung up and looked at the container of cinnamon rolls. At least he wouldn't have to give his up to Darius like he had thought he would.

Getting out of the car, he went in to see Frannie and Tony. He really hoped they might have an idea of what to do. They knew everybody in San Clemente and San Diego.

* * *

They'd just finished the treats Sophia had provided when a Drake took a call. He hung up, obviously upset.

"Was that your sister who called?" Frannie asked. Drake winced. He didn't want to lie, but he didn't want to have to explain either.

"Don't bother lying to her boy. I invented lying, and she invented sniffing them out," Tony DeLuca said as he hefted a bag of rice from a pallet onto the stainless steel kitchen island.

"Old man, you were supposed to let the youngster do the heavy lifting."

"As soon as a twenty-five pound bag of rice is heavy lifting, I'm going to the old folk's home," Tony quipped. "He gets to lift the fifty pound bags."

Drake kicked himself for not having gotten to the pallet before Tony.

"So was it your sister? The one with the three kids?"

"Four kids. Yeah, it was Maddie." Drake wished he could keep the worry out of his tone, but he couldn't.

"So when are you going back to Tennessee?"

"I'm not."

"Why not?"

"It's complicated. Right now my other sister is taking care of things. When she needs to call me in, she's going to. For now, it's better with me out of the picture," Drake said in a frustrated tone.

"I don't understand," Frannie asked, perplexed.

"Let the boy be, love. If he wants to tell us what's going on, he will." Drake looked around the food bank, and smiled. It was clean, efficient, but also welcoming, and it was because of the two people in front of him.

"You know, back in Ferris Holler our Food Bank wasn't nearly so well organized, and seeing as how half the town depended on it, you would have thought it would've been really well put together."

Frannie and Tony looked at one another.

"Did you donate your time there too, Drake?"

"Oh hell no, the Averys went there every Saturday and Tuesday to load up." Drake grinned. "You would have loved Miss Tilda, she ran the place. It might not have been organized, but the woman was a love to us kids."

"So speaking of love, tell us about Billy's girl. I want to be prepared. He's invited her to come help out at the pantry, and I want to know what to expect," Frannie said.

"I'm not telling you anything, Missy. You're going to have to come to your own conclusions." Drake turned to Tony with a bag. "Here are some special treats I almost stole to take home. However Sophia said she'd find out and beat me if I did."

Tony rubbed his hands together and peeked in the bag.

"Oooh, I love these." Frannie and Drake shared a smile.

* * *

Billy Anderson

Normally getting done with homework early was a good thing. Instead he found himself playing with his pie trying not to stare at Rebecca as she ate hers. Was a guy supposed to get turned on with the way a girl ate her food? She had ordered banana cream pie, and watching her lips part and savor the treat was making him ache.

The only saving grace was she had no clue he was stealing glances.

"Did you say your sister baked this pie?"

"She bakes everything in this diner," Billy said proudly. "Some gourmet stores in town want her to start producing baked goods for them as well. She's trying to figure out how to make it happen."

"Does she cook the food?"

"No, Peter does. She could, she's a great cook, but she's the waitress. To begin with she needed the tips so she could earn enough so I could come and live with her."

"I don't understand."

"I told you I was in foster care." Rebecca put down her fork and wiped her mouth with her napkin.

"I didn't believe you. I thought you were saying it to make me feel better."

"Rebecca, I would never lie to you." Billy looked her squarely in the eye.

"Good. It made me think less of you," she admitted. "Why were you in foster care?"

"My dad abandoned us when my mom got sick. When she got too sick to take care of me, I ended up in foster care. My sister worked herself to the bone to try to make enough to get a place good enough for me to come and live with her."

"Oh, that's a wonderful story." Rebecca was beaming.

"Why are you in foster care?"

"My mom is dead. My dad…" her voice trailed off.

Billy didn't say anything.

"They took me away from my dad when I was seven. I've been in and out ever since. He got me back once when I was ten. It didn't work out." He heard a wealth of pain in her voice.

"One family wanted to adopt me but he refused to give up his rights. I'm hoping if I get good enough grades I can get a scholarship to college and go early. I want to petition to be an emancipated minor."

Billy had never heard of someone so alone. That's what made him blurt it out.

"Rebecca, would you go with me to the Valentine's Day Dance." He watched as her eyes lit up, and she grinned. His heart soared. Then her whole manner changed.

"I'm sorry, I can't."

Billy mulled over the words. He'd seen the way she'd turned down Eric, and she'd had a lot to say, and at no time had she said 'she couldn't'.

"Should I ask why?" Billy questioned softly.

"I wish you wouldn't."

"Well, okay then." He reached out and held his hand up. It was the hardest thing he had ever done. But he got the feeling if ever someone needed a hug, or their hand held it was Rebecca Barnes.

She grabbed it and her grip was tight. She smiled at him. His heart soared again. He didn't know why she couldn't go, but it wasn't because she didn't like him. She did. And he got the distinct feeling it was more than as a friend. Jack and Clint had been right.

CHAPTER EIGHT

Sophia Anderson

Playing *Call of Duty* wasn't her idea of a fun night, but she appreciated the fact both Mason and Billy always invited her to join their game. These days what was really taking up a lot of her bandwidth was figuring out how to market the pies outside of the diner. Currently four different gourmet shops in San Clemente had asked her to bake product for them.

She wanted to do it, she had to figure out how to keep up the quality, and not sacrifice her home life. That meant she was currently looking at more resumes from Craig's list while listening to Mason and Billy.

"One of the guys I served with was an emancipated minor, it was a hard road. Rebecca has guts." She heard Mason say. Sophia stopped scrolling through the listings and started to pay attention to what was being said in the living room.

"How old was he?"

"I'm not sure."

"She says she wants to graduate from high school early and get a scholarship. I know her foster home isn't good. It isn't like being with the Bards," Billy said.

"It doesn't sound like you're mad at her for turning you down."

"No, she's too good of a friend. I'm bummed. But… well…it didn't feel like she was rejecting me. I kind of thought she wanted to go with me. I know it's probably wishful thinking on my part. I'm probably being stupid."

"Billy, I've known you for two years now. You're not stupid."

The doorbell rang.

"I've got it," Sophia called out as she grabbed her purse.

She checked the peephole before opening the door to the pizza delivery boy. She brought in the food to the dining room.

"Thanks, sis," Billy exclaimed as he put down his controller. Mason gave her a warm smile, and came to the kitchen to help her get the plates and napkins.

"So that's what's been going on, it's a girl, huh?"

"Isn't it always?" Mason asked as he stroked her hair.

"No," she replied. "Fifty percent of the time, it's a boy." He laughed.

"You heard?" Billy said as he came into the kitchen, and opened up the fridge. Sophia looked at her handsome young brother and gave him an encouraging smile.

"Yeah, I did. You okay with that?"

"I guess so. I got shot down. It was bound to happen, right?"

"Not in my book. I thought you were going to always have girls say yes, and be married by the time you were fifteen." He gave her a grin.

"You'd like Rebecca."

"Is this the girl from social studies?"

"Yep."

"Didn't you guys get an A? I like her already." The three of them sat down at the dining room table.

"She's nice, Soph. Real nice. You *would* like her."

Sophia looked at Billy in surprise.

"Billy, if you liked her enough to ask her out, I have no doubt in my mind I would like her."

Billy smiled in relief.

It suddenly hit Sophia how much of a stand-in she was for a mom. He really wanted her to like the girl he would bring home one day. She would always have to treat this with the care and dignity it deserved.

"Even though she's not going to go to the dance with me, I want to make sure she knows there are no hard feelings. I had asked if she had wanted to help out at the food pantry tomorrow and she had said yes. So we're still going to do that. Jack is going to pick us up."

"Would it be awkward if I was there too? Frannie had asked me if I could do some baking tomorrow at the pantry. She said there was a school carnival going on, and more people were going to need to pick up things at the pantry than normal." Sophia crossed her fingers underneath the table.

"No, it's cool. Like I said, you'll really like her. After all, she got me an A in social studies."

*   *   *

Mason had insisted on joining her saying he could help out with the pies. Bless his heart, he was good at many things, but baking wasn't one of them. As soon as they got to the food bank she suggested he help Tony and he jumped at the chance.

Even though Jack had picked up Billy before Mason and she had left that morning, they still weren't there. It was odd since Rebecca only lived five miles from the school.

Finally a grim faced Jack, a shaken Billy, and Rebecca showed up.

"Please don't be mad, Mr. Preston," Rebecca said.

"What?" Jack turned to the girl. "Honey I'm mad, but not at you, you know that don't you?"

She shook her head.

Billy stood beside her, and she took a step closer to him.

"I'm mad because they didn't provide you with a key and you spent the night outside on the porch."

"But you said I should have called someone—the police. So you're mad at how I handled it."

"No, he's not. He's like Drake. He has a code. He's being protective. Now he's going to go ballistic on their asses." Billy smiled at her, she bumped her hand against his, and he grasped it. She held on.

"Rebecca, I'm so sorry I said that. I wasn't thinking," Jack's voice was extremely gentle. "I should have realized how I would have come across to you. Thank you for being brave enough to speak up."

She looked at Billy for confirmation. He nodded.

She smiled at Jack. "I'm sorry for misunderstanding."

"There is absolutely nothing for you to be sorry about, it was on me. I was angry, but I should have made it perfectly clear it was at your foster parents for not taking care of you properly."

"It's no big deal. What's really important is they had the younger kids with them."

Sophia stepped forward.

"Hi Rebecca, I'm Sophia, Billy's sister. I have to say you're being very generous to the people who left you outside all night."

"They probably meant to leave a key under the mat." It was clear she was covering for them. Mason stepped up beside her. Rebecca's eyes got wide.

"Let me introduce you," Sophia said. "This is Mason Gault, he works with Jack. He's basically Billy's older brother."

"It's nice to meet you, Rebecca." Mason smiled.

"Drake told me about you. He said you would be mad at him if he didn't follow the SEAL code."

"What code is that?" Mason asked with an easy going grin.

"That you have to take care of women and children who are in trouble," Rebecca answered.

"He's right. If he doesn't follow it, he'd be in trouble."

"I thought he might be kidding."

"Oh no, it's real." Jack shared a smile with Mason.

"Rebecca, there's a place for you to wash up above the diner a couple of blocks away if you want," Sophia offered.

"There's no need," Billy said. "Jack got her into the house. She was able to shower and change clothes."

"Good man, Preston," Mason said.

"Rebecca, why don't you come with me? I need some help getting started on the pies I need to bake. The guys can start unloading the trucks and stocking the shelves. Do you bake?"

"A little."

"That's great. Frannie and I can use all the help we can get. And not from Mason," Sophia teased.

Rebecca looked at Billy for confirmation.

"It's true, she needs help and Mase sucks."

"Okay."

"You'll love Frannie," Billy assured her.

* * *

The three of them sat down and stared at the row of pies that lined the counter. Frannie looked at Sophia, then Rebecca, and back to Sophia.

"Oh my God, this is déjà vu all over again," Frannie said to Sophia.

"What?" Rebecca looked from one woman to the other.

"The similarity between you two girls."

"Us?" Rebecca said in shock.

"Oh yeah. It's like I'm looking at Sophia from two years ago."

"I don't understand," Rebecca said. "She's so much older than I am." Frannie shouted with laughter.

"You're right. She's ancient."

Sophia scowled.

"What could we possibly have in common?"

"What do you say, Sophia? Can I tell her your story? I think this little girlie is in dire need of some of the same help you needed back then."

"I think you're right, Frannie. Let's go outside where the guys won't overhear us."

They went out the front door since the guys were in the back unloading and putting the boxes and cartons away.

Frannie took a deep breath. "It's times like this I sure could use a cigarette."

"Well I'm glad you don't smoke anymore," Sophia said. "I want you around for a good long time."

"Look, Rebecca, I'm a bit of a buttinski," Frannie said. Sophia laughed.

"Actually she is a big one, and I thank God for it."

"This one came into the pantry thin as a rail. She needed food for her mama. All of the money was going to her mama's medicine."

"She was trying to figure out where she was going to live after her mother died."

"Probably a shelter," Sophia interjected.

Rebecca stared in shock.

"Things weren't going well but then she got a job at the diner. Margie gave her the apartment above it to stay."

"I don't understand? Why are you telling me all of this?"

"I'm getting there, girlie," Frannie said, taking another deep breath.

"This one," she said pointing to Sophia. "Well she meets Mason, and she decides she can't go out on a date with him because she doesn't have anything to wear. Sound familiar?"

This time it was Rebecca who took in a deep breath.

"How did you know?"

"Your clothes don't fit. Same as Sophia. You're looking at Billy like the sun rises and sets on him same as Sophia did with Mason. It was easy enough to figure out. I'm taking you shopping."

"I can't let you buy me clothes," Rebecca protested.

"It's the consignment store. It's good quality and used. And you don't have a choice."

Rebecca's eyes welled up.

"And you can't cry. I'm a buttinski."

"She is. I told you. A big one." Sophia nodded.

"Why are you doing this? Are you just doing this for Billy?"

"No honey, I'm doing this for you. Just like I did it for Sophia. I was your age once too. I didn't have a lot. Mrs. Woloceck helped me and I expect one day you do this for some other girl. We help others. It's what we women do."

"As for me, I've got something else in mind," Sophia said.

"What?" Rebecca asked.

"I've been scouring Craig's List for someone to help part time at the diner on the weekends. You can ask Billy. You proved you know your way around the kitchen. I need a helper with a good work ethic who can help me with the pies. It'll cut my prep time in half and give me more time at home with Mason. Want the job?"

"Are you two for real?"

"We've been in your too tight shoes, honey. Say yes." Frannie laughed.

"I really want to go to the dance."

"We know. Now say yes and go back inside. The store doesn't open for another hour."

"Yes!"

* * *

Billy Anderson

Billy stood beside Drake as he and they all looked at the pies lined up on the counter.

"It's time to move this show over to the diner," Mason said decisively.

"Now you're talking sense," Tony said. Frannie eyed him, and his shoulders drooped. "You go on ahead."

Sophia laughed. "We'll be back with cinnamon rolls for you, I promise. Plus an egg white omelet."

"Egg white," he whined.

"You like her egg white omelets, she seasons them up real good. Now quit your bitching." Jack and Billy laughed. Again Rebecca moved closer to him. It felt good that when she was uncomfortable or unsure she came to him for moral support.

"They don't mean anything by it," he whispered to her. "They're always like this."

"Are you sure?"

"Watch."

"Oh yeah, she puts the peppers and onions in with the Monterey jack cheese. I love those omelets." Tony nodded.

Frannie rolled her eyes, muttered something about men, and started to walk away.

"Now beautiful, don't go away in a huff. I just forgot. I love you women looking out after me, I really do." Frannie looked back over her shoulder and smiled.

"I want you around for a long time, old man." He went over and gave her a kiss on her temple.

"And I want as many years with you as I can get, Francesca."

Billy looked over at Rebecca and saw her wearing the identical sentimental smile as Sophia.

Mason put his arm around Sophia. "Time to go to the diner. I'm in desperate need of food."

"Good call, Mase," Jack said. "Who wants to drive with me?"

"We'll walk," Billy said. "If it's okay with you, Rebecca. It's only a couple of blocks."

"That would be really good," Rebecca said. "I wanted to talk to you about something anyway." Billy looked at her sideways. He hoped it wasn't anything bad. He was worried about what was going on at her foster home. If it was something bad he would convince her to tell Sophia and Mason. They could help.

"Rebecca, I'll be by the diner in an hour, don't forget," Frannie said.

"I won't," Rebecca said with a big smile.

Billy looked from one to the other.

"What's that all about?" he asked Rebecca.

"It's what I need to talk to you about. Let's go."

They walked out into the beautiful Southern California morning sunlight.

"It's just up the street about three blocks," he said as he guided her to the left. As they passed the first building, they caught sight of the ocean and they stopped to stare.

Billy looked at the curve of her face as the wind blew her long brown hair. God, she was pretty, and he could tell she had no idea.

"I really like your family."

"Mase and Sophia are great."

"I mean all of them. They *all* are your family."

She was right. They might not be family through blood or marriage, but they were family. Billy laughed.

"That finally explains Drake. Everybody is supposed to have one crazy uncle."

"Don't you mean the uncle everybody loves? Then there's Frannie, who is the fairy godmother."

"What do you mean?"

"I mean, if you still want me to, I can go to the dance with you...if you want." She bit her lip, her eyes hesitant.

Billy took a step to the side so he was standing directly in front of her, he brushed back a strand of hair the wind had blown into her eyes.

"Really Rebecca? Because taking you to the dance is really what I want. Are you sure?"

Her eyes twinkled and she grinned.

"I am absolutely positive I want to go with you, Billy Anderson!"

"Frannie had something to do with this?"

"She did."

"Then she's my fairy godmother too."

Chapter Nine

Drake Avery

Drake leaned against the counter, a cup of coffee in his hand, and watched as Sophia fluttered around Billy. He and Mason exchanged glances and headed towards the backdoor.

"God, Billy is a great kid. I think I would have told her to put a sock in it five minutes ago."

"You're so full of shit, Avery. You could no more have hurt her feelings than Billy would."

"She's worked on that tie of his four times. She should let you do it."

"It's important to both of them that she be the one to do it." Drake peeked in the kitchen window and saw them talking. Mason was right, you could see the connection between the brother and sister and how deep it was.

"I don't think I realized how much of a mother she's been to the kid."

"She's pretty damn special."

"You, Clint, and Jack are the lucky ones with the women you have. And if you fuck it up I'm going to hurt you."

"We know how good we have it. If we fuck it up, we're going to grovel to get back into our women's good graces."

"Glad to see the SEAL training has made you smart."

The door behind them opened.

"I'm ready, Mason." Billy was holding the container with the corsage. "It won't take long to get to Frannie and Tony's right?"

"Don't worry kid, you'll get there in plenty of time."

Drake still thought it was great Frannie had insisted on Rebecca coming over to their house to get ready. Those pieces of shit at the foster home weren't going to help her with her hair and make-up and all the girlie stuff like Frannie would.

Mason fished his keys from his jeans.

"You look good kid," Drake said.

Sophia beamed at her brother.

He watched as Mason and Billy got into the truck. God, the kid even walked like Mase.

* * *

Billy Anderson

"When we get there, I'm going to have her sit in the back of the crew cab with me. Does that sound right, Mase?" Billy rubbed his hands against his slacks.

"It sounds perfect."

Billy hated that he was nervous. He wanted to concentrate on Rebecca, not worry about how he felt. They pulled up to the DeLuca's house. He looked over at Mason.

"You'll do great." Mason gave him one last look of encouragement, and he got out of the truck.

Billy walked up the stepping stones but before he could knock on the door Frannie opened it.

"Billy Anderson, you look like a movie star." She dragged him in to the front hallway. "Stay right here. I wanted Rebecca to make an entrance," she whispered to him.

"Tony!" she yelled up the stairs. "Billy's here!"

"We'll be right down." Tony and Rebecca appeared at the top of the stairs. Time stopped. She looked totally different. Her hair. Her make-up. Her dress. But what took his breath away was the look of shy excitement in her eyes. She came down the steps with Tony at her side.

Tony brought her to a stop in front of him.

"You look beautiful," Billy said.

She smiled.

"I mean it, you're really beautiful, Rebecca."

Frannie pulled the corsage from his hand.

"I think this is for her, right?"

"Oh yeah. It's an orchid. For your wrist." Rebecca gave a wide grin and held out her hand. Frannie handed him the corsage and he slipped it on Rebecca's wrist. It was then he noticed the pink of the orchid matched the pink of her dress.

"Your dress is great, Rebecca." The sweetheart neckline and rhinestones at the waist made her look like a princess. She brushed down the satin pleats and looked at him through her lashes.

"Thank you."

"Now we need a picture." Frannie turned them towards Tony who had his phone pointed their way. Billy looked at Rebecca to see if she was okay with the idea. She looked over at him with a smile and reached out her hand.

* * *

Mason Gault

"Hey you two." He smiled as he let himself into the backdoor through the kitchen. How come I was pretty sure you'd still be here when I got back?" Mason asked Drake.

"Cause you're not stupid," Drake said.

Mason went over to the fridge and pulled out a Pacifico and sat down at the dining room table beside Sophia.

"Frannie sent me a text with a picture of the two of them. They looked adorable." She turned her phone around so he could see. It was nice, but they'd looked even better in person.

"So how long is a high school prom?" Sophia scowled at Drake.

"They're in ninth grade, you doofus. This is their Valentine's Day Dance. It'll be over in three hours."

"Well then I better tell you my news and leave you guys with some alone time."

"Is this about what Dare found out?" Sophia asked.

"I'm betting this is about his and Jack's mysterious absence today." Mason gave Drake a hard look.

"Like you wouldn't have gone with us if we'd invited you," Drake scoffed.

"What are the two of you talking about?" Sophia asked.

"Drake and Jack were AWOL for a few hours today. I'm suspecting they visited with Rebecca's foster parents. Am I right Drake?"

"We had a little meeting of the minds with those cretins."

"Am I going get a call from the authorities? Will you need an alibi?" Mason asked only half kidding.

"No. Mr. and Mrs. Yarbrough know better. And from now on Rebecca will have a key—not that she'll need it. Jack is one scary dude, Mase. He acts all Texas choirboy, but get him riled and he will make you remember the

Alamo. Anyway, he got Rebecca a phone with all of our numbers on speed dial. He explained to Yarbrough that if she should ever have a need to call us he and his wife will be wearing prison garb. I believed him, and more importantly, so did they."

"I hate that she has to spend one more day with them," Sophia said.

"Let me tell you what Dare told me," Drake said. "I talked to him this afternoon about the next steps with Rebecca. Unfortunately if they took Rebecca out of the home she's in today the only place they could put her is a group home. Same for the other kids with her. However, he said they are going to be easier to place because they're younger. Apparently people are faster to step up for younger foster kids."

"Sophia and I checked into getting certified and found out it's a long process. Then we thought about how awkward it would be with Billy."

Drake looked from one to the other and gave a slow grin. "Well I guess you *do* deserve *some* alone time."

"Fine, we're nice people. It still doesn't do shit for Rebecca. We've got to think of something," Mason muttered.

"Do you know who else checked into it? Finn's mom."

"Really?" Sophia asked. "That's wonderful."

"Yep. She's already applied. Darius said his friend is going to fast-track her application so she can take custody of Rebecca."

"Oh my God, for real?" Sophia got up from the table and hugged Drake.

"Your work here is done, Avery. Now give us our alone time," Mason drawled.

* * *

Billy Anderson

The girls left twenty minutes ago to go to the bathroom. He and his friends had tried to figure out why it always had to be done as a group activity. Then the door to the gym opened and he saw her. She floated into the room—there was no other way to explain it. Billy smiled to himself as Rebecca laughed at something Cammie said, and then she waved as she made her way over to him.

"Are you having fun?" he asked.

"I'm having a great time."

"This is for you," he said as he handed her the glass of punch he had poured for her.

"Billy, thank you for asking me to the dance tonight. I can't believe everything that's happened. Frannie and Tony. The way everybody's been so nice and has tried to help me. Your sister. Drake. It's all been so much and it's all because of you."

"Rebecca, you've got it wrong. They would have done it no matter what. They think you're wonderful and they're the type of people who help. They jumped in and helped Sophia and me when we needed it too."

"Jack gave me a phone with everyone's number plugged in. He said I should call if I ever needed help. I changed your number to the first contact," she told him shyly. His heart swelled.

"And if I'm not available you call one of the men. They're serious, they will come and help you any day, any time, no matter what. No more sleeping on the porch."

"I have a key now," Rebecca assured him.

"You also have us. We're not going anyplace."

"I still don't understand why."

"I didn't either for the longest time. It's who they are. It's their code." She opened her mouth to say something else, then stopped. Finally she said.

"I like their code, a lot." She ducked her head, then looked back up at him. "I like you too…a lot."

Billy swallowed.

"Have I told you how beautiful you look?" She did, too. She outshone every girl at the dance.

"You have, Billy, you've made me feel beautiful."

"Well good." He cocked his head as he heard the music change. "May I have this dance?"

He heard Cammie giggle but it seemed to come from a long way off. Rebecca gave a shy nod, and he escorted her across the floor. The gym had been transformed into a wonderland filled with twinkling lights and hearts. A new soft and low song started, and he finally got to hold her in his arms just as he had imagined all those weeks ago when he first thought about asking her to the dance.

Rebecca clasped her hands around his neck and laid her head against his chest. She was just the right height for him. He could smell the jasmine and vanilla scent of her hair. Gently they swayed together, until finally she pulled back a little and looked at him, her brown eyes liquid.

"Thank you so much for asking me to the dance tonight. It was more than I ever dreamed possible."

She licked her lips. Oh God, she'd glossed them.

Her fingers tightened on his shoulders.

Now he got it. This is what the guys had been talking about. She was giving him such a sweet signal, and it matched his every instinct.

He watched her carefully as he bent his head, and her eyes drifted shut, dark lashes dusted against her delicate smooth skin.

As his lips touched hers for the first time his eyes closed too. He savored the petal softness beneath his mouth and the hint of trembling strawberries.

Ever so slowly he drew back, and she opened her eyes. They stared, she grinned, and he knew his smile was equally wide. He wrapped her close into a hug.

"Rebecca, this is the best night of my life."

THE END

BIOGRAPHY

Caitlyn O'Leary is an avid reader, and considers herself a fan first and an author second. She reads a wide variety of genres, but finds herself going back to happily-ever-afters. Getting a chance to write, after years in corporate America, is a dream come true. She hopes her stories provide the kind of entertainment and escape she has found from some of her favorite authors.

Keep up with Caitlyn O'Leary:

Facebook: http://tinyurl.com/nuhvey2
Twitter: http://twitter.com/CaitlynOLearyNA
Pinterest: http://tinyurl.com/q36uohc
Goodreads: http://tinyurl.com/nqy66h7
Website: http://www.caitlynoleary.com
Email: caitlyn@caitlynoleary.com
Newsletter: http://bit.ly/1WIhRup
Instagram: http://bit.ly/29WaNIh

Books by Caitlyn O'Leary

The Found Series
Revealed, Book One
Forsaken, Book Two
Healed, Book Three
Beloved, Book Four (Spring 2017)

Midnight Delta Series
Her Vigilant SEAL, Book One
Her Loyal SEAL, Book Two
Her Adoring SEAL, Book Three
Sealed with a Kiss, A Midnight Delta Novella, Book Four
Her Daring SEAL, Book Five
Her Fierce SEAL, Book Six
Protecting Hope, Book Seven
(Seal of Protection & Midnight Delta Crossover Novel
Susan Stoker KindleWorld)
A SEAL's Vigilant Heart, Book Eight
Her Dominant SEAL, Book Nine (February 2017)

Shadow Alliance
Declan, Book One
Cooper's Promise, Book Two
(Omega Team and Found Crossover Novel
Desiree Holt KindleWorld)

Fate Harbor Series Published by Siren/Bookstrand
Trusting Chance, Book One
Protecting Olivia, Book Two
Claiming Kara, Book Three
Isabella's Submission, Book Four
Cherishing Brianna, Book Five

Made in United States
Troutdale, OR
07/02/2023

10931825R00070